P9-CRH-696

# Kylie Jean

## Spelling Queen

by Marci Peschke

illustrated by Tuesday Mourning

PICTURE WINDOW BOOKS
a capstone imprint

Kylie Jean is published by Picture Window Books
A Capstone Imprint
1710 Roe Crest Drive
North Mankato, Minnesota 56003
www.capstonepub.com

Copyright © 2012 by Picture Window Books

All rights reserved. No part of this publication may be reproduced
in whole or in part, or stored in a retrieval system, or transmitted in any form or by any
means, electronic, mechanical, photocopying, recording, or otherwise, without written
permission of the publisher.

Library of Congress Cataloging-in-Publication Data

Peschke, M. (Marci)

Spelling queen / by Marci Peschke ; illustrated by Tuesday Mourning.

p. cm. -- (Kylie Jean)

Summary: Kylie Jean is studying hard for the spelling bee at school, but she keeps
getting distracted by the kitten that she and her cousin Lucy found.

ISBN 978-1-4048-6801-4 (library binding) -- ISBN 978-1-4048-7212-7 (pbk.)

ISBN 978-1-4048-7616-3 (pbk.)

1. Spelling bees--Juvenile fiction. 2. Kittens--Juvenile fiction. 3. Cousins--Juvenile
fiction. 4. Schools--Juvenile fiction. 5. Texas--Juvenile fiction. [1. Spelling bees--
Fiction. 2. Cats--Fiction. 3. Animals--Infancy--Fiction. 4. Cousins--Fiction. 5. Schools-
-Fiction. 6. Texas--Fiction.] I. Mourning, Tuesday, ill. II. Title.

PZ7.P441245Sp 2012

813.6--dc23                                    2011029706

Creative Director: *Heather Kindseth*
Graphic Designer: *Emily Harris*
Editor: *Beth Brezenoff*
Production Specialist: *Danielle Ceminsky*

Design Element Credit:
Shutterstock/blue67design

Printed and bound in China.
010609R

For Amanda
with love for Rick
—MP

# Table of Contents

# All About Me, Kylie Jean!

My name is Kylie Jean Carter. I live in a big, sunny, yellow house on Peachtree Lane in Jacksonville, Texas with Momma, Daddy, and my two brothers, T.J. and Ugly Brother.

T.J. is my older brother, and Ugly Brother is . . . well . . . he's really a dog. Don't you go telling him he is a dog. Okay? I mean it. He thinks he is a real true person.

He is a black-and-white bulldog. His front looks like his back, all smashed in. His face is all droopy like he's sad, but he's not.

His two front teeth stick out, and his tongue hangs down. (Now you know why his name is Ugly Brother.)

Everyone I love to the moon and back lives in Jacksonville. Nanny, Pa, Granny, Pappy, my aunts, my uncles, and my cousins all live here. I'm extra lucky, because I can see all of them any time I want to!

My momma says I'm pretty. She says I have eyes as blue as the summer sky and a smile as sweet as an angel. (Momma says pretty is as pretty does. That means being nice to the old folks, taking care of little animals, and respecting my momma and daddy.)

But I'm pretty on the outside and on the inside. My hair is long, brown, and curly.

I wear it in a ponytail sometimes, but my absolute most favorite is when Momma pulls it back in a princess style on special days.

I just gave you a little hint about my big dream. Ever since I was a bitty baby I have wanted to be an honest-to-goodness beauty queen. I even know the wave. It's side to side, nice and slow, with a dazzling smile. I practice all the time, because everybody knows beauty queens need to have a perfect wave.

I'm Kylie Jean, and I'm going to be a beauty queen. Just you wait and see!

## Chapter One
# Easy as Pie

Mondays are spelling test days. So every Sunday night right before I go to bed, I have to practice my spelling words. Today is Sunday. I'm ready to go!

First, I get my spelling words list. Then I write all of the words five times each. Using a piece of notebook paper and a pink pencil, I write, "Pie, pie, pie, pie, pie." (Before I learned this trick, I wasn't a very good speller.)

When I finish writing down all the words, I decide to go to the kitchen for some of Momma's tasty apple pie. A is for apple. When I turn on the kitchen light, Ugly Brother is standing right in the middle of the room, waiting for some pie.

"Are you hungry for pie too?" I ask him.

He turns his head to the side and barks, "Ruff, ruff."

Two barks means yes. This does not surprise me one teeny tiny bit, since Ugly Brother is always hungry. I carefully scoot the pie plate off of the counter and onto the table. Then I scoop out a big messy piece of pie.

Plop! It lands in the middle of the paper plate. Then an idea hits my brain like cinnamon on toast!

Holding the plate, I suggest, "How about I get some pie for you and you help me study my words?"

Ugly Brother is already licking his lips. He barks, "Ruff, ruff."

I say, "We have a deal!" I put his plate on the floor and cut another piece of pie for myself. Ugly Brother eats his pie in two giant bites. Gobble! Gobble! Then he licks his plate.

When I'm done eating, Ugly Brother helps me with my spelling. I explain, "I'll spell the word. Then you bark two times if I'm right and one time if I'm wrong."

I put the list on the floor where he can see it. Then I start to spell. The words are: all, does, hid, people, find, sheep, book, train, jar, and pie.

The first three words are easy as pie, but then I have to spell people.

I spell, "P-e-e-p-l-e," and Ugly Brother barks, "RUFF!"

"You know what, I can spell that word," I say. "But that sneaky o gets me every time."

"What are you talking about?" T.J. asks as he walks into the room.

"Just a tricky spelling word," I reply.

T.J. puts half of the pie on his plate and pulls a fork from the kitchen drawer. He pours a big glass of milk to go with it.

"Are you trying to spell delicious?" he asks. "Because this pie is delicious!" He shovels the pie into his mouth.

"Momma would say you have bad manners," I tell him. "Even if you do think her pie is good."

T.J. ignores me. He asks, "Do you want me to help you study?"

Ugly Brother barks, "Ruff!"

That means no thank you. Picking up my spelling list, I head for the door. "No thanks," I reply. "I have Ugly Brother helping me."

Between bites, T.J. mumbles, "Suit yourself, Lil' Bit. You do know he's a dog, right?"

Clenching my teeth, I hiss, "Shhh. He thinks he's a real true person!"

Ugly Brother is already climbing the steps when I catch up with him. We study my words some more.

After a while, Daddy comes to tuck us in. He peeks around the corner and tells me, "Bedtime, princess."

Daddy kisses me on both of my cheeks and pulls the covers up to my nose, then kisses Ugly Brother on the tip top of his head.

As he turns out the light, I whisper, "I love you to the moon and back."

Daddy smiles and says, "I love you a bushel and a peck." He leaves the door open a crack, so the hall light can make a tiny glowing path across my bedroom floor. Then he tiptoes back downstairs.

## Chapter Two
# Super Spellers

The next day when I get to school, I sit down at my usual table with my best cousin, Lucy, and our friends Cara and Paula.

Paula seems really worried. She is very quiet, and Miss Paula Dupree is never quiet.

"Did you study for the test?" I ask.

She moans. "I forgot to learn the new words!" she whispers.

"Oh, no!" Lucy says.

"Don't worry," I say. "We'll help you with your spelling when we go to recess. Right, girls?"

Lucy and Cara are both super good spellers!

"Sure will," Lucy agrees.

"I know them all," Cara chimes in.

Paula sighs. "I sure hope y'all can help me learn the words extra fast," she says.

We all nod in agreement just as Ms. Corazón starts our morning math lesson. Math takes a long, long time. About fifty hours! Well, it seems that long, anyway.

I whisper, "Is that clock stuck? It's moving as slow as a possum at noon."

Lucy shakes her head. "No, it's right," she says. "We're the ones that are slow."

We do our practice problems. Finally, it's time for morning recess. Yay! We dash out the door, heading for the swings. Today we're lucky because there are four of us girls and four empty swings. Cole and the boys try to race for the swings, but we get there first. B is for boy.

Lucy has the spelling word list.

"I know all the words by heart," I announce, swinging high.

Lucy swishes past me. "Oh, good," she says. "I'll call them out, Paula can spell them, and you can check to see if she's right."

Cara asks, "What about me?"

I think for a second. Then I say, "You can remember the ones she misses."

We swing and spell.

Lucy swings out, calling, "All."

Paula says, "That's an easy one. A-L-L."

I swing in, shouting, "Ta-da! You're right!"

Every time Paula gets one right, we all cheer. Ta-da!

We keep on like that: swing in, spell, swing out, ta-da! It's a pattern, just like in math today.

"Don't forget the bonus word," I tell Paula. "If you miss a word, it can help you still make a hundred on your test!"

Paula says, "You are all the best friends ever. With your help, I think I'm going to make an A on this spelling test." She leaps off the swing and lands on her feet on the ground.

Back in the classroom, Ms. Corazón tells us to get out our paper and pencils. It is time for the spelling test.

Paula looks nervous, so I lean across our desks.

"Now, don't you worry," I tell her. "Just remember spelling on the playground. Swing, spell, ta-da! This test is gonna be as easy as p-i-e."

Paula nods. "I know, and pie is one of our words!" she says.

I whisper, "I know," and we all give Paula a thumbs up.

Ms. Corazón is ready. She will call out the spelling word, say it in a sentence, and then repeat it. We have ten spelling words. The word "ten" was on last week's list! Ms. Corazón says, "Sheep. Sheep live on the farm. Sheep."

I giggle. This is so funny, because Pa's Lickskillet Farm doesn't even have any sheep!

She keeps reading the words. I am pretty sure I spell them all right.

The bonus word is "letter." I know that one!

When the test is over, we each grade our own paper. I got every single one right!

Ms. Corazón asks, "Who made a hundred on their test?"

We all raise our hands, even Paula. That makes us all super spellers. Then I say, "I got the bonus word right, too. Ta-da!"

Lucy, Cara, and Paula chime in, "Ta-da!"

## Chapter Three
# The Cutest Cat

That afternoon, Lucy rides home on the bus with me. Usually her momma picks her up, but today she's getting her hair done at the Kut and Kurl beauty shop.

We hop up three steps to get on the bus.

Lucy says, "1, 2, 3."

I say, "A, B, C."

My favorite bus driver, Mr. Jim, puts his hand up. "Whoa," he says, and we stop.

He asks, "Does your cousin have a note from her momma to ride the bus?"

"Yes sir," Lucy says. She hands him the note and we go find a seat.

The girl behind us is writing a letter for her homework. Her name is Emily. She asks, "Hey, how do you spell 'dear'?"

I think about it. "Is it deer like the animal or dear like, Dear Lucy?"

"Not the animal one," Emily says, smiling.

Lucy says, "That's easy. D-E-A-R."

Lucy and I play tic-tac-toe on notebook paper. The bus gets louder and louder as more kids get on it. But once we start dropping kids off, the bus gets quieter and quieter.

When we get to Peachtree Lane, we hop down the steps to get off the bus.

Lucy says, "A, B, C."

I say, "1, 2, 3."

As we walk up the sidewalk, Lucy asks, "What do you want to do till my momma comes to get me?"

I'm thinking about her question. But then I hear something coming from the bushes right by the front door. "Meow, meeooow." I look at Lucy and Lucy looks at me!

She asks, "Did you get a cat?"

"No, not yet, but maybe I'm getting one today!" I say. I throw down my backpack and circle the hedge, calling, "Here, kitty, kitty. Come on out. I want to be your friend."

Lucy watches me. She's not sure about a strange cat that we don't even know yet. She frowns and says, "Maybe we should go get your momma."

Just then I see part of the cat under the bush. "No," I whisper. "It's a beautiful little cat. I'm sure it's very nice, so would you please help me catch it, Lucy?"

We both get down on our knees in the grass, peering under the bushes. Suddenly we see the cat. I squeal. It's a cute little kitten! It's a tiny white ball of fur, with a sweet face, a little pink nose, and a black patch over one eye.

Lucy leans back. "I wonder where the momma cat is," she says.

I throw myself down on the ground, and then crawl like a spider right up under that bush and rescue the poor baby cat. Then I carefully inch my way back out, holding the little kitten close to keep it safe.

Lucy is shocked! The number one beauty queen rule is to not get dirty, and I am covered with dirt like a monster truck at the mud bowl.

I hand the kitten to Lucy so I can dust myself off. Once my clothes aren't dirty anymore, I reach out and say, "Give it back now."

Lucy shakes her head. She says, "I'm going to be this kitten's momma."

Now I'm shocked! After I went to all the trouble to get that kitten, Lucy is trying to be its momma instead of me.

I think fast. "Lucy, I love you, and you are my best cousin," I begin. "But I just saved that cat, so I am the momma."

Lucy starts to cry. I feel bad. Too bad we didn't find two kittens. Then an idea hits my brain like summer catfish in a hot skillet. Since we only have one, we'll have to share it!

I put my arm around Lucy's shoulder. "I have an idea," I tell her. "We can both be the kitten's momma!"

She sniffs. Then she asks, "Where will our baby cat live?"

I think about it for a minute.

"Well, sometimes the kitty can live in the country with you," I say. "And sometimes it can live in town with me."

Lucy is cheering up, and she hands the kitten to me. Just then, Momma comes out and cries, "Where on earth did you get that cat?"

"I found it in our yard in the bushes because it wants to live with me, and Lucy too sometimes," I say. "Please let us keep it, Momma. This baby kitten needs us!"

Lucy adds, "Please, Aunt Shelly!"

Momma takes the cat and looks it over real good. "This is a girl kitty," she says. Then she asks, "Does she have a name?"

Lucy and I look at each other.

I say, "Princess."

She says, "Patches."

Momma looks at Lucy. "You'll have to do some fast talkin' to get your momma to let you have a cat," Momma says. "She doesn't even like cats."

Lucy frowns. "I know my momma will love Patches," she says. "Please?"

"I'm still not convinced we need a cat," Momma says. "What about Ugly Brother?"

"Well, he would like a little sister," I tell her. "I just know it."

Momma thinks for a while. I hop from one foot to the other, over and over. Finally, Momma says, "You can keep the kitty if Lucy's momma says it's okay, if you promise to look after it, and if Ugly Brother can get used to having a cat around."

Lucy and I squeal and hug each other. Then we hug Momma.

"Thank you, Momma!" I say.

Momma smiles and hands the kitty to us.

"Can we please please please name her Patches?" Lucy asks me. "Pretty please?"

"Okay," I say. "If we can put a pink collar on her."

Lucy smiles and nods. "That'll be fine," she says. "Just fine!"

## Chapter Four
# Be in the Bee?

As soon as we get to school on Tuesday, Lucy and I tell everyone about Patches. When we see Cara and Paula we shout excitedly, "We have a kitten!"

Cara smiles. "Two new kittens? How fun!" she says. "They're going to be best friends."

I shake my head. "Just one kitten," I explain. "We're going to share her."

"What's her name?" Paula asks.

"It's Patches," Lucy tells her. "I picked it out. Isn't it the cutest name ever?"

"Princess would have been better," I say. "She is the cutest little white cat with a black patch over one eye. That's why Lucy decided her name should be Patches."

"Take your seats, class," Ms. Corazón says. "I have an important announcement!"

I am not sure what could be more important than a new kitty, but I go straight to my seat anyway. Beauty queens are not rule breakers, and they always follow directions.

Ms. Corazón explains, "Next Monday, we will be having a class spelling bee. The winner will get a blue ribbon and then be in the school-wide spelling bee."

The whole class hums with excitement as our teacher passes out a practice list of words. This is exciting because I am a fantastic speller now. But it's not exciting because practicing for the spelling bee will be a lot of work.

When we go to the cafeteria for lunch, Paula is pushing peas around on her lunch tray because peas are not her favorite. Today they have fried chicken, peas, salad, and a roll. I brought my lunch in my pink lunchbox. It has lots of pretty little hearts all over it.

I say, "Y'all, help me think. Should I be in the bee? What's good about the spelling contest? What's bad? Is it the kind of thing a beauty queen should do?"

Lucy points out, "There isn't really a spelling bee queen, so there's no crown."

Cara says, "I think it's good practice for talking in front of a lot of people. Beauty queens have to be good talkers."

Paula adds, "Even if you don't get to wear a crown, it's probably okay to wear your best pink dress. You would get a blue ribbon if you win."

I take out my thermos. Then I pour my tomato soup with ABCs into a little bowl. As I stir, a Y pops up, then an E, and a S.

I can't believe it, but there is a word in my bowl! I shout, "My soup says yes! Besides, everyone knows beauty queens have to be smart too, so I just have to be in the bee!"

Together we look at the list of words to study. Some words are so hard, like "orange," and some are so easy, like "six."

Paula says, "You might need help with the hard words. We'll all help you study, just like you helped me!"

I wink at my friends. They're the best friends in the whole wide world! "I knew I could count on y'all," I tell them.

The big yellow lunchroom is noisy, but we start to practice anyway. They call the words and I try to spell them. Lucy puts a star next to the ones I still need to study some more.

I can't wait to tell Momma, Daddy, T.J., Ugly Brother, and Patches all about the big spelling bee!

* * *

That night at the dinner table, I tell everyone
my news.

Except Patches. I can't tell her because she's
not home. I keep forgetting that she lives at Lucy's
house sometimes.

I say, "Today, our teacher told us that we're
going to have a spelling bee. I think I'm going to
sign up."

"Sugar Pie, since I taught you my secret spelling
trick, you're a fantastic speller," Daddy says. "You
should go right on ahead and sign up for that
spelling bee."

"I think I will, Daddy!" I say. "I think it could
be real fun."

Momma pours everyone sweet tea except me. I get pink lemonade. Y'all know pink is my color.

Everyone talks about their day. I stop and think about spelling each word I say.

Ugly Brother hangs out under the table until I feel sorry for him and sneak him a tasty bite of dinner. Daddy winks at me. He sneaks Ugly Brother bites, too!

T.J. tells me, "If you're going to be in the bee, Lil' Bit, you better let a person help you study instead of our dog."

I say, "Shhh. Remember, he thinks he's a real true person!"

Ugly Brother hears anyway! He barks, "Ruff, ruff!"

"Well, you hurt his feelings," I say. I eat fast. Then I say, "Can I be excused?"

"What are you going to do?" Momma asks.

I tell her, "I need to study more words!"

# Chapter Five
## Grocery Store Speller

Early, early Saturday morning Momma and I go to do the grocery shopping at the Piggly Wiggly. In the backseat, I spell words all the way there. I start with an A word. Always. B word. Before. C word. Crisp. I keep going till I get to Z for zoo!

When we finally get to the store we park in the giant parking lot with the yellow stripes. It's already half full of cars, vans, and trucks. Momma waves to our neighbor Miss Clarabelle as she picks a grocery cart.

Momma asks, "How are you, Miss Clarabelle? Your flowers sure are pretty this time of year."

Miss Clarabelle replies, "I'm fine. How are y'all doing? You know, I could use some help with my flowers. Maybe Kylie Jean can come help me pull some weeds later today."

Momma chooses a grocery cart. "We're all just fine. Thank you for asking," she says. Then she winks at me. "And Kylie Jean would be happy to help you weed your beautiful garden."

"Yes, I would!" I say.

First, Momma and I go to the fruits and vegetable section. I see lots of fruits and veggies. Big piles of pretty red tomatoes are stacked up, but I bet they don't taste as good as Pa's, fresh from the farm.

We finish in that part of the store lickety-split because we get most of our fruits and vegetables from Lickskillet Farm. Momma gets all of her herbs from Granny.

Next, we go to the butcher. He cuts the meat at the Piggly Wiggly. Momma gets hamburger, chicken, and steaks. She uses the steaks to make chicken fried steak, but they don't really have any chickens in them.

They have flour on the outside and Momma fries them in her big old black skillet. You can't flour a rich steak. Daddy cooks those on the grill!

After a while I get bored and say, "Hey, Momma, let's race!"

Momma shakes her head. "I don't think so," she says. "How about we play a game instead?"

"What kind of game?" I ask.

"A spelling game," Momma says.

That doesn't sound as fun as racing, but I'll give it a try. "Okay," I say.

As we walk along, putting canned goods, cereal, bread, and milk into the cart, Momma calls out words for me to spell. She says, "Spell dairy! And don't look at the sign!"

I spell, "D-a-i-r-y. Did I get it right?"

Momma cheers. "Yay! You did."

I tell her, "We like to say ta-da, not yay."

Momma says, "Okay, then, ta-da!"

She asks me to spell cereal, pie, and cupcake. All those words are on the second grade spelling bee practice list.

"Some of these words are pretty hard for a second grader," Momma says.

I nod. "Yes ma'am," I say. "That's why I need to practice all I can."

We keep loading up the cart and marking off our grocery list. In the cereal aisle, we really pile up the boxes. T.J. can eat a whole box in two days! I get a box of cereal with ABCs in it.

"Now you can practice while you eat your breakfast," Momma says.

Momma only shops every two weeks, so before long, we can hardly see because we have so many groceries piled up high.

Momma crosses off the last thing on her list. Then she says, "Come on, darlin'. We have one more aisle to go to before we check out."

This is so weird! I thought we finished the list.

We cross the store and turn down the pet aisle. Right in front of me is a whole section for cats.

They have cat food, cat toys, and cat collars. I see a pink collar!

I shout, "Oh, Momma, I just love that pink collar with the little diamonds and the big bow! Can I please buy it for Patches?"

"It sure is beautiful," Momma says. "But I'll have to take some money from your allowance. Okay?"I nod, holding the perfectly pink cat collar.

Momma says, "Now it's time to check out, sweet pea."

When we get to the front end, we go straight to Miss Bea's lane to check out. Miss Bea is real nice to me.

As Miss Bea scans our cans, I say, "Miss Bea, I'm going to be in a spelling bee."

"Are you really?" she asks.

Putting cereal boxes on the counter, I add, "I just said three Bs in one sentence: Bea, be, and bee."

Miss Bea stops scanning our groceries. "Aren't you something?" she says, smiling at me. "Can you spell orange?"

"No problem for me. I'm a fantastic grocery store speller," I brag.

After I spell orange, Miss Bea gives me a Piggly Wiggly sticker for each hand. After all, I had to spell a super hard word! Momma laughs and shouts, "Ta-da!"

Miss Bea scans the pink collar for Patches. I tell her, "That cat collar is for my new kitty, Patches. My cousin Lucy and I are her new mommas because she lost her real momma."

"That's real nice," Miss Bea says. "Thank you for shopping at Piggly Wiggly."

Then we have to hurry home and put all the groceries away before Lucy and her momma, Aunt Susie, bring Patches over.

It's my turn to have the kitty. Lucy got the first week, so we could have time to explain to Ugly Brother all about how he was going to get a little cat sister.

"You're really gonna like your new cat sister," I tell Ugly Brother while we wait for Lucy. "She's real nice."

Ugly Brother doesn't look too sure. Then I say, "You have to look out for her just like T.J. looks out for me. Okay?"

Ugly Brother stares at me. Then he barks, "Ruff, ruff."

But he doesn't really sound like he means it. I don't know if he's ready for a sister. I sure hope he is nice to her today, because being a big brother is a very important job!

When Lucy and Aunt Susie come into the kitchen, Momma is putting away the last box of Fruity-O's.

"Hello!" Aunt Susie says. "We are bringing this baby cat back to its other momma."

I run over to grab Patches. Lucy hands her to me. I hold the kitty up and give her a little kiss.

Patches licks my face. It tickles a little. Her tongue is kind of rough and scratchy.

Ugly Brother is under the kitchen table. I tell him, "Come say hi to your little sister."

He barks, "Ruff." Then he lies right down and closes his eyes. How rude! I just know he's not sleeping.

Lucy is not sure what to think. She asks, "Does Ugly Brother know Patches is going to stay here tonight?"

I shrug and say, "Well, I told him more than once. Wait until you see the new collar I just bought for her!"

I hold up the collar and Lucy gushes, "Ooh! I love it!"

Momma and Aunt Susie have a nice visit while Lucy and I play with Patches.

Momma says sisters always have things to talk about. I sometimes wish I had a sister, but being a cat's momma is pretty fun, too!

## Chapter Six
# Pull and Spell

Later that afternoon, Miss Clarabelle calls to
see if I can come over and help in her garden.
Momma says yes.

She finds Patches and me in the back yard.
We are stretched out swinging in the hammock.
Patches is purring, and I'm reading a book called
How to take Care of Your Kitten.

Momma asks, "Sweet Pea, are you ready to go
help Miss Clarabelle in her garden?"

"Yup!" I answer. Then I tumble out of the hammock. Patches flies out and lands in the soft grass. She starts meowing.

Ugly Brother sees me on the ground and runs over to play, but when he sees Patches, he barks.

I shout, "Ugly Brother, you be nice to your baby cat sister!" Then, in a quieter voice, I say, "It's not time to play right now anyway. We've got to go help pull weeds."

Ugly Brother puts his head down. He knows I don't like it when he's mean to Patches.

I hand Patches to Momma. "Can you babysit Patches while I go pull weeds?" I ask.

"I sure can," Momma says. Then she and Patches head inside.

I go into the garage and get my basket, my hat, and my pink gardening gloves. Then I walk over to Miss Clarabelle's.

She is working on the flower beds in her back yard. There is a big pile of weeds on the ground next to her. I push them over. Then I sit down by her, pulling on my gloves.

"Why, hello, Kylie Jean!" she says. "Thank you so much for coming over to help me."

Under the orange lilies are thin, tiny green sprouts. The best thing to do is pull them out carefully so you get the roots too. If you don't get the roots the weeds grow right back.

"I see you have some weeds here," I say, looking at her flowers.

Miss Clarabelle smiles. "Yes, I do," she says. "And you are just as sweet as sugar to come and help me."

That gives me a great idea. "Can we practice spelling while we pull weeds?" I ask.

Miss Clarabelle replies, "That's a marvelous idea. You help me and I'll help you. Can you spell flowers?"

I spell, "F-l-o-w-e-r-s. Flowers."

Once I get that one right we just keep right on pulling weeds and spelling words. I spell spider, ant, plant, leaf, daisy and dirt. My pile of weeds is getting really big.

Ugly Brother has been sniffing around. I call, "Ugly Brother, come and help us."

He runs over and I load my pile of weeds into the basket I brought over.

I tell him, "Take these weeds over to the trash pile. Okay?"

He barks, "Ruff, ruff." Then he picks up some of the weeds in his teeth and takes off. I see some of the weeds fall out of his mouth as he runs.

Miss Clarabelle notices too. She smiles at me and says, "Maybe carrying weeds is not the best job for Ugly Brother."

"He can't pull weeds, either." I remind her. "Remember how he tried to eat them the last time I helped you?"

Miss Clarabelle laughs. "Oh, my! How could I forget?" she says.

We talk about the spelling bee and then I tell her all about Patches.

Miss Clarabelle is a good listener. That's a good thing, because I'm a good talker. Ugly Brother listens too.

Miss Clarabelle asks, "When will it be your turn to take care of the baby cat?"

"It's my turn to be Patches's momma right now," I say. "Momma is babysitting her while I'm here helping you."

Suddenly I miss that baby kitty so much I just want to go home. Miss Clarabelle looks at me. "You must miss her," she says. She looks around. "I think we're about done here, Kylie Jean, and you've been a big help to me. Why don't you head home now?"

I hop up and run away, calling, "Goodbye, Miss Clarabelle!"

## Chapter Seven
# Fun at the Farm

After church on Sunday, the whole big family is meeting at the farm for dinner. Except for Ugly Brother. He is not getting along with his little cat sister, so he has to stay home. It just breaks my heart.

Before we leave, I tell him, "I've told you a hundred times that I don't love Patches better than you. Please don't be jealous, so you can come to the farm, too!"

Ugly Brother barks, "Ruff!"

He has started barking whenever Patches is around. Barking dogs and cats don't mix, so we have to leave him behind.

When we finally get to Nanny and Pa's, I pull off my church clothes as fast as I can. In two seconds flat, I'm dashing out to the barn in my play clothes.

"Lucy, you in here?" I call as I make my way into the dark, sweet-smelling barn.

"I'm back here," she yells. Lucy is at the end of the barn looking for something.

Some of the horses shift and make soft noises as I pass by the stalls. There's a new colt in the last stall. It is black with wobbly legs.

Lucy says, "Come help me look for our old baby buggy."

"Did you see the new little h-o-r-s-e?" I ask her. "What's Pa going to name it?"

Lucy looks confused at first. Then she says, "Oh, I get it! You're practicing for the spelling bee. I did see it! It's so cute. Maybe they could name it Midnight."

As I get closer to the back of the barn, Patches starts to meow. She climbs up on my shoulder. Her tiny claws are kind of sharp. I guess she hears Lucy talking and is trying to see her other momma.

"Okay, I'm here to help you look," I tell Lucy. "I think they should name that colt Licorice. Pa's favorite candy is licorice. What are we going to do with the buggy when we find it?"

Lucy points to a big purple bag on the ground. There are some baby doll clothes spilling out.

I spell, "C-l-o-t-h-e-s." Then I ask, "Are we going to play dolls?"

"No, silly!" Lucy exclaims. "Those are for our sweet little kitty, Patches. I know she wants to look really cute, so we're going to dress her up in style."

Patches meows loudly. She looks funny wearing her fancy collar in the barn .

Suddenly, I feel nervous. "Do you think she can get hurt when we change her clothes?" I ask Lucy. After all, my job as Patches's momma is to see to it that she never gets hurt or goes hungry.

"No way," Lucy says. "Daisy dresses her cat up all the time!"

Now I'm getting excited. I try to imagine our Patches in a precious pink baby doll dress.

"You know what?"
I say. "She is going
to look like a p-r-i-n-c-e-s-s
all dressed up."

Just then I see a tiny
corner of the pink baby
buggy. It's poking out of one of
the empty stalls on the other side of the barn.

Pointing, I shout, "There it is!"

Our old doll stroller is stuck under a bunch of
junk. First, Lucy pulls on the buggy. After I put
Patches down, I pull. Then we both pull together,
trying hard to get it out.

Finally, the stroller rolls right on out. It shoots
out so fast that we both fall down laughing.

A bunch of old junk tumbles out behind it. Old watering cans, pool floats, egg baskets, and milk pails litter the barn floor. I stand up and dust myself off.

"We better clean this m-e-s-s up before Nanny sees it!" I whisper.

Lucy nods. We start stacking up the junk and shoving it back in the stall. When everything is put away, I suddenly remember our kitty.

I spin around and look at the spot where I put her down. It is just a dab of dirt without any little white fluffball sitting on it.

I scream, "Where's Patches?"

"I thought you were taking care of her!" Lucy says.

"I was," I say sadly. "But I put her down to help you with the buggy."

Lucy calls, "Patches, Patches! Come here, sweet little kitty!"

I feel as bad as a dog without a bone. I'm a terrible cat mother! Patches is lost and I don't know where to look. All around us are big horses that could scare an itty bitty baby cat.

"Maybe she's hiding from the horses, and she's too scared to come out," I say. "We should check in some good hiding spots."

Lucy shouts, "You can't take your eyes off a baby. Do you think she could get out of the barn by herself?"

I shake my head. Now I want to cry!

Lucy says, "If you really loved Patches you wouldn't lose her!"

That makes me feel even worse.

Then I hear a faint little meowing sound.

"Shhh! Hear that?" I ask.

Lucy says, "It's coming from the junk pile!"

Patches's tiny face pops out of a watering can. We both dash over, but I get there first.

I gently pour Patches out of the can and give her a great big hug. "Thank goodness you're safe," I say, nuzzling her little face. "We thought you were lost, but since we found you, I am the happiest girl in the whole wide world!"

Lucy is just itching to get her hands on our cat. "Come on, Kylie Jean," she says. "It's my turn to love on her and you lost her, so give her to me!"

I feel real bad about losing Patches, so I hand her over to Lucy for some kisses.

After that, we dress our kitten in a little pink dress with white lace and bows all over it. It has a little bonnet to match and looks nice with Patches's special pink collar.

Lucy puts a baby blanket in the buggy for Patches. It is as soft as a spring cloud. Then we carefully put our baby cat in the buggy so we can go show her off.

The buggy bounces along the dirt path from the barn to the farmhouse with Patches peeking over the side to see what is going on.

Pa sees us coming. He hollers, "Well, what do we have here?" We push the buggy close so he can see better. When he peeks inside, Pa grins and his eyes twinkle with laughter. "That's a beautiful little cat baby!" he says.

"Yes sir, we know," I say. Then I remember my manners and add, "and thank you kindly."

"Are y'all taking good care of your baby?" Pa asks.

Lucy says, "Yes sir!"

Then we both push the buggy down the hill to show everyone else our little princess.

*Chapter Eight*
# Bad Dog

Finally, the big day arrives! It's time for the class spelling bee! As soon as I wake up on Monday morning, I start practicing spelling my words for one last time. While brushing my teeth, I spell a word. "S-h-i-n-e." Then I ask, "Ugly Brother, am I right?" and he barks, "Ruff, ruff."

I put on my best pink dress. Downstairs, Momma brushes my hair. I spell a word, t-o-g-e-t-h-e-r, as I hold Patches in my lap.

Daddy says, "Fantastic, sugar pie!"

"Thank you, Daddy," I reply, smiling.

Momma says, "Put that cat down before you go to the table."

I set Patches on the floor. Then I pull up a chair at the kitchen table next to T.J. He is stuffing pancakes in his mouth. I sip some orange juice. Momma makes my pancakes look like ABCs. Then she spells a word on my plate. It says l-o-v-e!

Suddenly from under the table we hear, "Meow, meow, meow!" It sounds like Patches is in trouble!

I shout, "T.J., did you step on my baby cat?"

T.J. looks shocked and says, "Hey, I didn't do it!"

I jump out of my chair and look for Patches. Peering under the table, I see Ugly Brother, but I don't see Patches.

Then I hear a meow that sounds like a whisper. Where is my baby cat? That's when I notice that Ugly Brother has two tails, and one is long and white!

"Oh no!" I yell. "Ugly Brother is sitting on Patches. Help!" I try to grab Ugly Brother's legs and pull him up. "You're being a bad dog! Get up before you squish Patches!" I tell him.

T.J. grabs Ugly Brother by the collar, dragging him out from under the table. Patches looks up at me with big eyes and cries, "Meeooowww!" Momma kneels down beside me, picking up Patches.

"Is Patches okay?" I ask, trying hard not to cry.

Momma says, "She's not hurt. She's just scared."

T.J. shuts Ugly Brother in the laundry room. Momma looks at me and says, "Kylie Jean, I think you better let Patches live with Lucy. You can always go visit. Ugly Brother just can't get used to having a little sister."

Now I can't stop myself from crying.

T.J. says, "It's almost time for the bus."

Daddy gives me a big squeezy hug. "Just calm down, sweetheart," he says.

"I don't want to go to the spelling bee," I say. "I don't think I'll be able to spell my words when I'm crying."

"Oh, hush," Daddy says. "You can do it."

"I have been practicing and practicing," I say, sniffling, "so I would hate to miss it."

Daddy smiles. "I have a prediction," he says. "You want to hear it?" I nod, and Daddy says, "You're gonna win that spelling bee today!"

Then I think of my poor little baby cat and I start to cry all over again. Ugly Brother could have hurt her really bad. Lucy would never forgive me!

I feel awful. Even though I'm still really sad, I grab my backpack, lunchbox, and homework. Then T.J. and I head outside to wait for the bus.

On the bus, I sit on the seat right behind Mr. Jim, our bus driver, so that I can tell him all about Ugly Brother sitting on Patches and today's spelling bee.

"Hey, Mr. Jim," I say. "My dog tried to sit on my cat! Today I'm going to be in my class spelling bee, but I'm so worried about Patches I don't know if I can remember how to spell my words."

Mr. Jim smiles. "I'm sorry about your cat," he says. "And good luck with your spelling bee."

"Oh, I don't need luck," I say. "I know all the words. Do you want me to spell them all for you right now?"

From the back of the bus, T.J. shouts, "Mr. Jim, please just say no. She really means it!"

Mr. Jim nods. "That's okay, Kylie Jean," he says. "I believe you can spell them all."

## Chapter Nine
## Class Bee

When we get to school, I go straight to my classroom. I have to tell Lucy about Ugly Brother and Patches. Maybe she'll be happy since our baby is going to have to live at her house.

As soon as I walk into the room, Lucy asks, "How is our baby cat?"

I take a deep breath. "Well, she's okay now," I say. "But Ugly Brother sat on her today! Please don't be mad. She's not hurt too bad, just scared."

Lucy gasps. "Are you sure she's okay?" she asks.

I reply, "Yup, cross my heart. And the good news is, Momma says Patches has to live at your house all the time now."

Lucy grins. "Well, you can come see her whenever you want," she says. "She'll always be your kitten too."

I smile. Lucy really is my best cousin.

"Are you ready for the spelling bee?" she asks.

I tell her, "I know all my words by heart."

After the bell rings, it's time to start the bee. My tummy is full of hummingbirds. I try to take deep breaths while I wait for my first word.

Ms. Corazón says, "Kylie Jean, please spell 'sister.'"

Sister is a great word because Ugly Brother has a little sister kitty now. Even if he doesn't like her. I say, "S-i-s-t-e-r."

Daisy gets "orange." It is kind of a hard word. Some kids think the g is a j, and Daisy gets it wrong. Ms. Corazón says, "I'm sorry, Daisy. You are out. Please sit down."

Cara gets "shape." She spells it right. I want to shout, "Ta-da!"

Next Lucy spells "S-m-a-r-t." She is so smart, she gets her word right.

I'm a little nervous. But you won't believe it — my next word is "kitten"! Of course I spell it right!

Cara gets "grandfather." I hold my breath for her. She spells "G-r-a-n-d-f-a-t-h-e-r."

Now it's Lucy's turn. Her word is "balloon."

She starts, "B-a-l . . ." but then she stops. She asks, "Can you please say the word again?"

Ms. Corazón says slowly, "Balloon."

Lucy takes a deep breath and spells, "B-a-l-o-o-n."

Ms. Corazón smiles kindly and says, "I'm sorry, Lucy. That was incorrect. Please sit down."

One by one, more students have to sit down. Soon, only Ryan and I are still standing. Ryan gets the word "between." It could be a hard one to spell, but he gets it right.

When it's my turn, I think of all the words I still don't know how to spell. Yikes! Luckily, I get the word "cookie."

Whew. That is a very easy Piggly Wiggly word. Being a grocery store speller helps me get it right. We are both still in the contest.

Ryan's next word is "hobby." He spells, "H-o-b-b-e-y." I want to jump up and down like a jack rabbit. He added an extra letter!

Ms. Corazón smiles at me and asks, "Kylie Jean, can you spell 'hobby' correctly? If you can, you'll be our class winner!"

I spell, "H-o-b-b-y."

"Correct!" Ms. Corazón exclaims. "You spelled your word with no mistakes. Now you will go on to the big bee on Monday with the all the students in first through fifth grade at our school."

I throw open my arms wide and shout, "Ta-da!"

My friends cheer, "Ta-da!"

Ms. Corazón pins a big blue ribbon to my shirt.
It says "First Place Speller" in gold letters. It's not a
tiara, but I like it!

I can't wait until after school so I can show Mr.
Jim, Momma, Daddy, T.J., and Ugly Brother my
big blue ribbon!

## Chapter Ten
# Some Speller

That afternoon, when Mr. Jim sees my
first place spelling bee ribbon, he says,
"Congratulations! You must be some speller, little
lady."

"Yes sir, thank you very much," I say. "And
now I'm going to be in the big spelling bee next
Monday."

At home, I show Ugly Brother. I know I should
be mad at him because he was mean to Patches,
but I love him too much.

Besides, he is real proud of me and he wants to lick my ribbon. I tell him, "No licking the ribbon!" but I let him lick my face and give me some sugar.

Momma makes a special afternoon snack for me because I'm the winner. She says, "Blueberry Pop-Tarts for a blue ribbon winner."

We are still in the kitchen talking about being blue ribbon winners when Daddy comes home from work. He sneaks a bite of my Pop-Tart. I say, "Hey, that's my snack!"

Then he sees my big ole first place blue ribbon and says, "See, Sugar Pie, I knew you were going to be a fantastic speller!" Then he gives me a big squeezy hug.

"Your prediction came true, Daddy," I say.

Then Daddy spells, "P-r-e-d-i-c-t-i-o-n."

* * *

The next day is Saturday. As soon as I wake up, I pin my first place ribbon on my shirt. Downstairs, Momma is fixing cereal.

"Aww, I thought you were making eggs and bacon for breakfast today," T.J. complains.

Momma shakes her head. "Tomorrow I'm making a big breakfast," she explains, "so today we're having cereal."

She puts a box of Fruity-Os and a gallon of milk in front of T.J.'s bowl. I see that Momma already has a bowl of ABCs cereal ready for me.

"Thanks, Momma!" I say. "I love to eat alphabets! Yum!"

After I eat my breakfast, I spend all day practicing my spelling. I can play and practice at the same time. When I jump rope, I call out letters each time my feet skip over the rope. I jump and call out letter D, jump and call out letter R, jump and call out letter E, jump and call out letter A, jump and call out letter M.

Ugly Brother watches me. I tell him, "I just spelled 'dream.' You know that ever since I was an itty bitty baby it's been my dream to be a beauty queen."

He barks, "Ruff, ruff." I lay down the rope and give Ugly Brother my best beauty queen wave, nice and slow, from side to side.

I love my baby cat Patches, but now it's just like the old days, just me and Ugly Brother.

I use my sidewalk chalk to spell all the big words I have been learning on the driveway. I write the really big words with my pink chalk.

When T.J. comes home from football practice, he can tell I'm ready for the big bee. He says, "Looks like you're ready to spell."

I grin and spell, "Y-u-p!" The letters tumble right off my tongue and T.J. laughs.

After T.J. goes inside, I ask Ugly Brother, "Do you think I can win the big bee?"

He barks, "Ruff, ruff!"

That means yes!

## Chapter Eleven

# The Big Bee

On Monday morning, I am ready! I have on my lucky pink dress. As Momma kisses me goodbye, she says, "I know the big bee is from nine to eleven in the school auditorium. I'll be there!"

"Okay, Momma!" I say. "See you later!"

I am so excited that I can hardly sit still on the school bus. Mr. Jim looks in his rear-view mirror and says, "If I didn't know better, I'd think you were sittin' on a pile of fire ants, little lady!"

"Today is the big spelling bee and I'm in it," I remind him. "I even wore my lucky pink dress just in case I need some luck."

"Betcha won't need it," Mr. Jim says.

When we get to school, Cara, Paula, and my best cousin Lucy are waiting for me. Ms. Corazón is letting them help me practice one last time before the bee.

We go to the playground and swing and spell. They ask me the words.

When I get them right, my friends say, "Ta-da!"

Lucy says, "Spell family."

I spell, "F-a-m-i-l-y"

My friends all shout, "Ta-da!"

We keep on practicing. I spell owl, planet, spin, bread, jump, uncle, globe, and sheep.

Then Ms. Corazón comes to the door. She shouts, "Come in, girls! It's spelling bee time."

We yell, "Okay." Then we jump out of our swings and run for the door.

It's nine o'clock on the dot. Ms. Corazón leads our class into the auditorium so we can sit with all of the other second grade students in the two front rows. Then she helps me fix the bow on my pink dress. It must have come loose when I was wiggling on the bus.

Ms. Corazón tells me, "Win or lose, all I can ask is that you do your very best, Kylie Jean."

I take a deep breath. Then I reply, "Yes ma'am, you know I will. And when I do, I'll be as happy as a pig in mud!"

All of the contestants line up to go on the stage. I find my seat. It has a white paper taped to the back with my name on it, Kylie Jean Carter. I sit right on down. The chair is kind of tall and my feet swing back and forth.

I am a little anxious to get started. Next to me, Billy Joe from first grade looks like he just swallowed a bug. I decide I should tell him my teacher's advice. I give him a thumbs up and whisper, "You're gonna be just fine. Win or lose, just do your best."

He looks like he feels a little better. Then our principal welcomes everyone and now I know we're about to get started. I look out into the dim auditorium and I can barely see Momma in the audience. I give her a quick little beauty queen wave, side to side. Then I put my hands back in my lap.

I whisper to Billy Joe, "Did you know they don't like dogs to come to school even if they're your brother?" He looks shocked!

One of the teachers, Ms. Shay, will call out the words. After she says the word, you can ask her to say it again or say the definition.

Ms. Shay gives me the word "sailboat." I ask her to say it again while I try to remember if it's one long word. Then I spell, "S-a-i-l-b-o-a-t."

She says, "Correct!"

Other kids spell their words. Then Billy Joe gets his word. His word is "green." He goes and gets it right.

Ms. Shay says, "Correct!"

Beside me, Billy Joe gives a great big sigh. "Whew."

The round is over. All of us got our first word right.

In the next round, the third grader misses her word and is out. Poor Billy Joe gets his word wrong and is out, too. He looks like he's going to cry. That means it's just me and two other kids.

My word is "whiskers." It is a strange word. What if I get it wrong? I'll be out of the bee!

Then I remember the cute kitty's picture on Patches's bag of cat food. Suddenly, I can see the word in my mind.

I get it right, and I'm still in the contest! After all, I did practice at the Piggly Wiggly. I'm a real true grocery store speller, so I know my food words.

Momma claps and cheers, "Ta-da!"

We start the next round. The fourth grader gets his word, "wobble," right. The fifth grader gets the word "yesterday." It's a long one, so she takes her time. I can see her chewing her lip. She is thinking hard before she spells it. Once she does, she gets it right.

I get the word "horse." I am lucky because I love horses. Of course I get my word right.

The fourth grader gets the word "nickel." He says, "N-i-c-k-l-e—" Then he covers his face with his hands. He knows he spelled it wrong. Up until he mixed up the last two letters, he had it right. I think he was just nervous!

Now the fifth grader stands up.

Ms. Shay says, "Please spell 'opposite.'"

The fifth grader spells, "O-p-p-o-s-i-t, opposite."

That sounds right to me, but Ms. Shay says, "I'm sorry, that is incorrect. If Kylie Jean can spell the word, she is the winner."

I blurt out, "I bet I can spell that word!"

Ms. Shay says, "Go ahead, Kylie Jean, and spell opposite for us."

I stand up tall, thinking about the sneaky e like at the end of the word "people." That has to be the mistake that fifth grader made.

I call my letters out as loud as I can. "O-p-p-o-s-i-t-e, opposite."

"I just left out one letter?" the fifth grader says. He moans. "No fair."

Ms. Shay turns to the audience and announces, "We have a new spelling bee champion, second grader Kylie Jean Carter! She will represent our school in the county-wide spelling bee at the end of the month."

She presents me with a beautiful trophy.

It is a golden cup with
ABCs around the bottom
and on the front it says "Big
Bee, Spelling Winner." It
looks like a tall cup with
handles on both sides. It
is not a tiara, but I like it
anyway.

Everyone in second grade
is chanting my name. "Kylie Jean! Kylie Jean!"

Momma is waiting beside the stage to give
me a big squeezy hug. I hold up the trophy so
Momma can see. She laughs. "Kylie Jean, you are
a super speller."

I say, "Ta-da! I knew I could do it, Momma!"

When I get home that afternoon, I run all the way from the bus to the front door as fast as I can!

After I slam the front door, I holler, "Ugly Brother, come quick! Ugly Brother!" He runs toward me. We sit together on the floor by the front door so that I can show him my spelling bee trophy. Ugly Brother sniffs it and licks the outside of it.

"Don't you just love my ABC spelling bee trophy?" I ask.

He barks, "Ruff, ruff!" Then he tries to fit his nose inside the trophy cup.

I know just what he's thinkin'. I laugh. "Silly Ugly Brother! We can share this trophy, but no eating out of it! Okay?"

Ugly Brother barks, "Ruff, ruff."

Then I add, "We're gonna share this trophy with Miss Clarabelle, T.J., Momma, and Daddy. They all helped me learn to spell."

I pet Ugly Brother and he licks my face. That means he likes my idea. Sharing makes a person good on the outside and on the inside. Just like Momma always tells me, pretty is as pretty does.

"Ugly Brother, I sure wish they had spelling bee queens," I say. "Can you spell queen?"

He barks once, "Ruff." That means no.

I spell, "Q-u-e-e-n."

Ugly Brother barks twice and licks my face. "Yup! That's me," I say. "Kylie Jean, the Spelling Bee Queen!"

**Marci Bales Peschke** was born in Indiana, grew up in Florida, and now lives in Texas with her husband, two children, and a feisty black-and-white cat named Phoebe. She loves reading and watching movies.

When **Tuesday Mourning** was a little girl, she knew she wanted to be an artist when she grew up. Now, she is an illustrator who lives in South Pasadena, CA. She especially loves illustrating books for kids and teenagers. When she isn't illustrating, Tuesday loves spending time with her husband, who is an actor, and their two sons.

# Glossary

**announcement** (uh-NOUNSS-muhnt)—something said in front of a group

**bee** (BEE)—a contest

**buggy** (BUG-ee)—a baby or doll stroller

**convinced** (kuhn-VINSSD)—sure, believing

**correct** (kuh-REKT)—right

**delicious** (di-LISH-uhss)—yummy

**fantastic** (fan-TASS-tik)—wonderful

**jealous** (JELL-uhss)—wanting what someone else has

**marvelous** (MAR-vell-uhss)—wonderful

**practice** (PRAK-tiss)—repeat something over and over until it is done right

**prediction** (pri-DIKT-shuhn)—a guess about the future

**trophy** (TROH-fee)—an award given to a winner

**Talk!**

1. Lots of people help Kylie Jean, and she helps lots of people. Who do you think was the most helpful? Why?

2. Kylie Jean practiced hard to learn all of her spelling words. What are some good ways to learn hard things?

3. What do you think happens after this story ends? Talk about it!

# Be Creative!

1. Kylie Jean's goal is to be a beauty queen. What's your number-one dream?

2. Who is your favorite character in this story? Draw a picture of that person. Then write a list of five things you know about them.

3. Kylie Jean was proud to become the spelling bee champion. Write about something you did that you are very proud of.

This treat is just the thing to eat after a long day of spelling. Y-u-m-m-y!

*Love, Kylie Jean*

## From Momma's Kitchen

HONEY BEE SPELLING SURPRISE

YOU NEED:

Honey (1 tbsp per person)

Alphabet cereal (1/2 cup per person)

Plain or vanilla yogurt (8 oz per person)

Your favorite berries (1/4 cup per person)

1 clear glass for each person

1. Spoon honey into the bottom of each glass.

2. On top of the honey, add a layer of yogurt and a layer of berries. You can use thinner layers and repeat, or just do big thick layers.

3. On top of the yogurt and berries, add alphabet cereal. Finish with a drizzle of honey and a few more berries. Serve immediately.

# THE FUN DOESN'T STOP HERE!

## Discover more at www.capstonekids.com

- ♥ Videos & Contests
- ✿ Games & Puzzles
- ♥ Friends & Favorites
- ✿ Authors & Illustrators

Find cool websites and more books like this one at www.facthound.com. Just type in the Book ID: 9781404868014 and you're ready to go!